STEVIE NICKS
ROCK'S MYSTICAL LADY

STEVIE NICKS
ROCK'S MYSTICAL LADY

Edward Wincentsen

Wynn Publishing

WYNN PUBLISHING
P.O. Box 1491
Pickens, SC (29671)
U.S.A.
864-878-6469
www.wynnco.com

First Printing, July 1993
Second Printing, March 1995
Revised, Expanded Edition
Third Printing, February 1998

© 1993, 1995 Edward Wincentsen
Library of Congress Catalog Card Number: 93-91523
ISBN: 0-9642808-1-7

Associate Editor: John Wooley
Book Design: Ed Wincentsen
Typesetting: Marc Mathers

Dedicated to
Jean

Who's help at the
very beginning
was invaluable

A gypsy heart
gone
too soon.

Introduction

T O SOME, Stevie Nicks symbolizes the un-
tamed gypsy; to others, the searching spirit, the
seeker of the Holy Grail. Her music and image
present her as dreamer and visionary, someone who
doesn't always fit within the boundaries of ordinary
life. She often seems to be from another age and
time. Critics have accused her of being too far "out
there," of having her head in the clouds. But haven't
the same criticisms always been said of poets, mystics
and artists?

Stevie's preoccupation with spiritual searching is
reflected in her songwriting, which gives her
listeners glimpses of her questions, quests and
discoveries as she follows her unique path through
life. At times, this path appears to be made up of
such incompatible elements as Eastern Mysticism,
New Age thought, occult teachings and Christianity.
Perhaps these are not conclusions at all, but spiritual
hypotheses, for her to test and to accept or reject as
she travels further down her path.

I do not wish to speculate on Stevie's beliefs.
I do want to say that I, along with many other
admirers, relate to her search and find inspiration
from her path.

Stevie has often said that Taylor Caldwell's
Ceremony of the Innocent is one of her all-time

favorite novels. Its message of lost innocence may have helped fuel Stevie's desire to see innocence live and triumph, a position she takes in such songs as *After the Glitter Fades*. Another recurring message in her work seems to be that we should keep on believing in the good, the holy and even in the impossible.

After listening to many hours of demos and unreleased songs done by Stevie Nicks, I came away amazed by her songwriting skills. These raw recordings, most with only minimal instrumental backing, show her tremendous talent for both lyric and melody. In fact, sometimes the finished, highly-polished tracks tend to obscure her songwriting ability, even though her searching spirit still shines through.

What future direction will this artist take in her journey through life, and in the lyrics and music that reflect that journey? Will we, her listeners, continue to be challenged and inspired by her poems set to music?

Whatever the future holds for this original talent, I think that it can be said that her audience will always be there for her, eagerly waiting for new works and inspiration.

Prologue

ON May 26, 1948, Stephanie Lynn Nicks was born in Phoenix Arizona's Good Samaritan Hospital. Just down the road from the hospital, between Phoenix and Scottsdale, is a mountain called Camelback Mountain, so named because of its resemblance to a camel's hump. There's a rocky protrusion on one side called the Monk, which often traps unwary adventurers who get up it and can't get back down. Helicopter rescues are commonplace on the Monk.

As a little girl, Shephanie Lynn Nicks told people she knew how to get both up and down the Monk. The mountain was her mystic friend and inspiration.

¤

When Stephanie Nicks was very young, she had trouble pronouncing her first name, so she called herself Stevie. By the time she was five, she was already an extrovert, dancing for hours in front of a mirror and sometimes joining her musician grandfather, A.J. Nicks, at one of his country-music gigs. He even crafted a small guitar for her.

At sixteen, Stevie composed her first song about a lost love. This new dimension of songwriting was an additional element of satisfaction and inspiration and gave her the strong motivational force that she would later need to survive in the tough world of the music business. In high school she became a part of a four-piece folk-rock band called the *Changing Times*.

A longtime musical collaboration began when she met Lindsey Buckingham while she was still a high school student. Together they formed a group called the *Fritz Memorial Band*.

Stevie graduated from high school in the '60s, a revolutionary time for music, politics and life styles in America. Enrolling in college as a communications major, she continued to perform in *Fritz,* and the band began opening for a number of the new groups that were exploding onto the San Francisco rock scene.

One of these was *Big Brother and The Holding Company,* with its electrifying lead vocalist, Janis Joplin. The soon-to-be legendary rock singer's flamboyant image and personality impressed young Stevie. She was especially taken with the ability Janis had to hold an audience in the palm of her hand.

But perhaps an even bigger influence on Stevie from those days was an unnamed flower child who attended one of *Fritz's* shows. "I saw this girl in the audience wearing a mauvy pink chiffon skirt and very high cream (colored) suede boots," Stevie recalled. "Her hair was kind of Gibson — she had some pink ribbons — and I thought, that's it."

Stevie's image and persona was born, a pure Pre-Ralphaelite mystic flower child.

STEVIE NICKS
ROCK'S MYSTICAL LADY

Stevie Nicks
Rock's Mystical Lady

EVEN AS a child, Stevie Nicks was undoubtedly nudged toward a career in music by her musician grandfather, A. J. Nicks. Her mother was also a big influence, especially about the lyrics her daughter would later write. According to Lydia Carole DeFretos writing in the December 11, 1985 *Aquarian Arts Weekly,* Stevie's "fascination with the land of make-believe and dreams was instilled in her by her mother. Barbara Nicks told her daughter countless tales of fantasy and fairy tales when she was growing up."

Stevie's fondness for exploring the mystical in her songs puts her in the company with other contemporary songwriters. There's Van Morrison, who began exploring a mystical territory in the '60s with his Irish band, *Them,* and continues in the same vein today. His Irish temperment sometimes whetting his spiritual lyricism to a hard edge.

Donovan, always the poet, put mysticism into '60s electric music with the LPs *Mellow Yellow* and *Sunshine Superman*. Both albums spin the same sorts of mysterious musical webs that Stevie has become famous for. Cat Stevens, another mystic minstrel, captivated audiences of the '60s and '70s with his unique words and music. Bob Dylan has had his moments of mystical inspiration, as has Britain's Kate Bush, who began reaching American audiences in the late '70s. And the Canadian Leonard Cohen's lyrics contain many mystical connotations.

In a 1981 interview for the February '89 issue of *Muscian,* Stevie told writer Timothy White, "I love the mysterious, the fantastic. I like to look at things otherworldly and say, 'I wonder what goes on in there.'" In commenting, White wrote, "Ms. Nicks remains a believer in ghosts and witches, a devotee of the occult who is capable of conducting entire conversations about the modern import of Halloween (her favorite night of the year), the usefulness of the Tarot, and the significance of maya, which in Hindu embodies the illusory world of the senses."

Patricia Kennealy, in her recent autobiography, *Strange Days, My Life With and Without Jim Morrison*, which centers around her time with the volatile Morrison, wrote that she, herself, was and still is a witch. Numerous magazine articles in the past have speculated that Stevie is also a witch. Citing among other things, the mystical subject matter of many of her songs, as well as her onstage persona. Stevie has often said that she is attracted to magic, and subjects related to nature and the elements.

Photo: Nancy Barr-Brandon

But simply being attracted to magic doesn't make a person a witch, and some contend that the study and practice of "Wicca" is in no way wrong or "evil." Stevie has referred to herself as a witch in the past, but it's hard to tell if she really means it. In a televised conversation with MTV veejay Mark Goodman, for instance, she said she'd "lied" when she called herself a witch. "Or," she added, "just in the funny sense... like the silly witch that crashes into your window on a broom."

That was in 1984. Two years earlier, in the March 1982 issue of *High Times,* writer Liz Derringer asked Stevie about her fascination with witches. Stevie replied, "I dream only about giving a little fairy tale to people. My fantasy is giving a little bit of the fairy princess to all the people out there that maybe don't have the Hans Christian Andersen books, and the *Grimm's Fairy Tales.* If that's the only thing I can do for them, well, that's fine."

In the same interview, Ms. Derringer commented that she couldn't imagine Stevie as "a type that sits around and puts black spells on people."

"I don't do that," responded Stevie. "That's silly and stupid, and anyone that does that is making up their own character and has nothing to do with me."

At the very least, Stevie is a person keenly attuned to the world beyond the physical. A person who has claimed on at least two occasions to have had experiences with the spirit world.

Her first experience was mentioned in a reminiscence for the British publication *Woman's Own* magazine, telling of her friend Robin Anderson's death from leukemia and her subsequent marriage to Robin's husband, Kim. Robin and Kim had a baby boy, Matthew, and Stevie said that she realized the marriage was wrong when Robin gave her a sign from beyond the grave. "I had got used to going in and finding (Matthew's) cradle rocking without anyone being there and I always knew it was Robin," Stevie related. "But on this occasion it wasn't rocking, nor the next day either, and that was when I realized she had finally left."

"Somehow, I knew she was telling me, 'You'd better get out of this right now. Kim will take good care of Matthew, but this is not what God meant for you, Stevie.'"

Speaking to writer Timothy White, this

time for an excellent 1981 *Rolling Stone* piece called *Stevie Nicks' Magic Act,* Stevie related the story of a "good ghost" haunting the Le Chateau in France, where she and the other members of *Fleetwood Mac* were recording. Among the manifestations were the sounds of flapping wings, doors swinging open by themselves, lights flashing back on after they were turned off, and something brushing against Stevie's cheek in the darkness. When she found out from the Le Chateau staff that the ghost was "good," White said she told the others, "If the ghosts are friendly and willing to talk, I am ready to sit down at any time. I would love to."

Stevie's song *Rhiannon* not only helped propel *Fleetwood Mac* to international superstardom, it also reinforced the aura of mysticism surrounding Stevie Nicks. In the April 1976 issue of *Phonograph Record*, she said, "It's freaky, but people will come up to me every place we play and tell me what an effect *Rhiannon* has had over their lives, as if it has some spiritual power over them... I wrote the song about a Welsh witch on the piano two Octobers ago, then Lindsey (Buckingham) and I joined the band on New Year's Eve, and both the song and the band have been evolving ever since. There's definite mystical implications."

In another *Rolling Stone* article, Daisann Mc-Lane wrote about seeing Stevie pull out a photograph of herself "onstage with the rest of *Fleetwood Mac,* in her witch costume" and saying, "This is Rhiannon, without a doubt." Later in the story, Stevie told Ms. McLane that Rhiannon "is some sort of reality. If I didn't know she was a mythological character, I would think maybe she lived down the street."

¤

Backstage at the Gramy Awards

Photos (4): Nancy Barr-Brandon

27

Photo: Nancy Barr-Brandon

28

Photo: Nancy Barr-Brandon

An early concert after Stevie and
Lindsey Buckingham joined Fleetwood Mac.
8/31/75, Balboa Stadium, San Diego.

Although *Rhiannon* provides a good example of
Stevie's love for the mystic and mythological,
there are apparently some areas she says to beware
of. In her MTV interview with Mark Goodman,
she talked about the dangers of otherworldly con-
tact, something especially relevant in these days of
New Age "channeling."

"I think you can summon things that you
shouldn't mess with," she explained. "There are
mischievous spirits around."

Photo © George Kane

Yet, author, Jeff Godwin finds that statement contradictory. This writer judges much of the material in Godwin's book *Dancing with Demons: The Music's Real Master* extreme, to say the least. But Godwin does bring up a controversial opinion about Stevie's song *Gold Dust Woman.*

First, some background on the song itself. In his book *Fleetwood, My Life and Adventures in Fleetwood Mac,* drummer and band co-founder Mick Fleetwood talks about how sickly and frail Stevie seemed to be when the band recorded *Gold Dust Woman.* He writes that she "began to draw within herself, reaching inside for the magic." The lights were dimmed, Stevie was sitting in a chair surrounded by "a Vicks inhaler, tissues and throat lozenges," went through seven takes of the song before capturing "the mysterious power and emotionality," Fleetwood says they wanted.

It was 3 A.M. Perhaps they captured something else then as well.

In the November 1976 *Crawdaddy,* Stevie said *Gold Dust Woman* is about "groupie-type ladies who stand around and give me and Christine (McVie) dirty looks, but as soon as a guy comes in the room are overcome with smiles." Her lyrics, as printed on the record, tape, and CD liners, seem to reinforce this. The printed lyrics

paint an unflattering portrait of one of the back-stage staples of the rock 'n roll life, reflecting Stevie's dislike of this particular type of person.

But the recorded *Gold Dust Woman* contains other lyrics as well that are not printed. Towards the end of the song if you listen very closely, you'll hear additional lyrics that go something like this:

> *Great shadow of demon*
>
> *Black widow*
>
> *Hail shadow of dragon*
>
> *Gold dust woman*
>
> *Hail shadow of woman*
>
> *Black widow*
>
> *Hail shadow of dragon.*

Jeff Godwin believes that "hail," used in this context, means "come forth," as in an evocation, a calling forth of spirits. He also alleges that these particular words, which Stevie sings to Mick's changing drumbeats, are part of a witchcraft incantation. Did Stevie, as Godwin contends, slip a little on this

particular occasion, ranting her anger at groupies with the help of "mischievous spirits?"

Perhaps she did and perhaps she didn't. There is, however, no doubting the role that the study of mysticism plays in Stevie's life and art. Metaphysics, defined by Webster, is the branch of philosophy that seeks to explain the nature of being and reality. Mysticism is defined as the belief in direct or intuitive attainment of communion with God or spiritual truths.

Books she has reportedly studied include the three-volume *A Course In Miracles*, published in 1976 by The Foundation For Inner Peace, headed by parapsychology investigators Robert and Julie Skutch. Dictated to Columbia University psychologist Helen Schucman by an "inner voice" that claimed to be Jesus, it presents the philosophy that guilt is absolved through forgiving others, and aims to correct what it says are errors of traditional Christianity.

Other books of reported importance to Stevie include *Sacred Symbols Of The Ancients,* which, according to its publisher's catalog, tells of "the mystical significance of our 52 playing cards and their amazing connection with our individual birthdays... an invaluable adjunct to the use of the Tarot in linking the most individual details of our lives to the cosmic whole." Then there's *In God's Way,* written by a psychic, and *The Diary of a Drug Fiend,* by the infamous Scottish occultist, Aleister Crowley. Stevie has allegedly given friends copies of this book, explaining that she doesn't support Crowley, but only wants to help her friends with any drug-dependency problems.

Crowley (1875-1947) lived a life that was rife with controversy, dying a debt-ridden drug addict. But *The Diary of a Drug Fiend* is actually a statement, in novel form, of Crowley's thoughts on how to overcome any habit or addiction through self-discipline, as well as his belief in what he called "The Law" or "Principles of Thelema." Writers Israel Regardie and P.R. Stephensen, in their biography *The Legend of Aleister Crowley,* defined the Law of Thelema's main principle: "That each individual should ascertain his True Will and do it. The new religion urges that 'Every man and woman is a star, i.e., a unit of cosmic significance and autonomy... Do what thou wilt — a command from gods to man — is the summary of the Law, which is to replace the Thy will be done — an entreaty from men to God — of earlier religions."

Stevie Nicks doesn't appear to embrace this particular philosophy. In fact, as she told Timothy White in *Stevie Nicks' Magic Act,* she sometimes confides in "the unknown God, whoever he or she is. I don't go to church, but I am very religious. I was raised Episcopalian, but I went to Catholic schools here and there. I love Gregorian chants, and I write chant structures..."

¤

41

The Hollywood Star
Walk of Fame Ceremony

Photos (3): Nancy Barr-Brandon

Photo: Nancy Barr-Brandon

Photo: Nancy Barr-Brandon

47

Photo © George Kane

S TEVIE has said that Christine McVie, her *Fleetwood Mac* cohort, has been like a mother figure to her. Interestingly enough, Christine herself has had her own experiences with the mystical and psychic. She told Timothy White for a February 1989 *Musician* story, "My mother, Beatrice Perfect," was "a remarkable, very psychic lady... a medium and faith healer. Her strange talents and interests used to concern me, because she belonged to these psychic research societies and would go off ghost hunting. As for her faith-healing, I had a rather nasty wart underneath my nose when I was about eight. My mother just put her finger on it one night before I went to bed and when I woke up the next morning it was gone."

Stevie Nicks not only deals with mystical subjects in her songs, sometimes the very songwriting process itself is full of the mystic and unexplainable. In the August 1982 *Mademoiselle,* she told writer Jon Pareles, "Somebody is waving a magic wand for sure over this whole thing," adding that she believed in "wonderous coincidences" and that "little magic things give me terrific ideas."

She also believes in dreams as a source of inspiration. Her first solo album, *Bella Donna,* is a good example. The design of the photo images on the LP's front and back covers came to her in a dream. "I dreamed that I saw, against a background of blue, a white vertical line, which was me holding a bird," she told Timothy White. Later, in her dream, she said, she picked up a tambourine and roses, "and I'm looking through the crystal tambourine, which symbolizes a porthole, to see the sorrows of the world. I love the symbolism of the three roses, which is very pyramid, very Maya."

According to one of Stevie's associates, Glen Parrish, the number three holds great significance for her. In the book *Everything You Wanted to Know About Stevie Nicks,* he stated that she believes in Tarot cards, astrology, and a "force and a feeling that makes things happen." Stevie, explains Parrish, composes songs because of these beliefs and because she believes that songwriting was what she was meant to do. From this, we can infer that Stevie — like Van Morrison — is very much an "inspirational" songwriter, in that inspiration must come before she can write a song.

Where does Stevie Nicks' inspiration come from? Sometimes it comes from her favorite writers and poets, as she related to Jenny Boyd, Mick Fleetwood's former wife, for Ms. Boyd's book *Musicians In Tune.*

"Sometimes I'll get out of bed in the middle of the night and go into my office and put the paper in the typewriter and get out my books that are inspirational to me — Oscar Wilde, Keats, Canadian poets, European poets — and I'll just open a page and read something, and I'll say, 'Okay, this is my information for today, this is what is supposed to come through me today,' and I'll close the book, so I'll never be able to find that page again, and I'll think about it for awhile, and then I'll probably write for one or two hours, then I'll be able to go back to bed."

At times, her inspiration is helped along by co-writers, including Mike Campbell of the

Heartbreakers. As Stevie told Redbeard and Joe Rhodes of the *Album Network,* "I'll probably tell Michael more secrets than I tell most people. So we have this little mystic thing, this little secret between us and our songs. It's like a baby, something that you make together, and it's really precious to both of us."

Occasionally, the circumstances that inspire her creativity are less positive, as was the case with *Edge of Seventeen,* a song she wrote following the deaths of her uncle Jonathan and music

great, John Lennon.

"The line 'And the days go by like a strand in the wind' — that's how fast those days were going by during my uncle's illness, and it was so upsetting to me," she told Timothy White (as quoted in *Stevie Nicks' Magic Act*). "The part that says 'I went today... maybe I will go again... tomorrow' refers to seeing him the day before he died. He was home, and my aunt had some music softly playing, and it was a perfect place for the spirit to go away. The 'white-winged dove' in the song is a spirit that is leaving a body, and I felt a great loss at how both Johns were taken. 'I hear the call of the nightbird singing come away... come away...'"

Wherever the inspiration comes from, Stevie appears to believe that there are unseen forces always lending her a hand. "I feel there are good spirits everywhere when I'm writing my songs, helping me," she told Sylvie Simmons in a *Creem* interview. "I just feel them and feel good."

Perhaps that helps explain the positive nature

Photo: Joe Sia

of much of Stevie's songwriting, her emphasis on the good rather than the bad. When asked by Timothy White what "come in from the darkness," (the phrase on *Bella Donna's* back jacket) meant, for instance, she said, "The dark side of anyone, the side that isn't optimistic, that isn't strong." And, again talking with Sylvie Simmons — this time for *Raw* — she added, "I don't write real happy songs, but I don't ever write a song that leaves people with no hope. I don't want somebody to walk away from one of my songs

Taj Mahal, Aug. '92.
Little fan, Jessica and her
uncle meet Stevie backstage.

L to R: Christopher (Stevie's brother),
Stevie, Barbara (Stevie's mom).

feeling bad. I want them to say, 'Well, she went through a difficult experience but she came out of it and she's okay, and if she got through then I can get through too.' That's mostly why I write..."

"Everything I write comes from reality," she added, "and then I throw a handful of sparkle-dust over it and try to make it so that people can accept it and say, 'Life goes on no matter how bad or what kind of tragedy you're involved in.' I'm telling you that I've been through it all and I'm still here."

¤

Certainly Stevie Nicks has had her share of tragedies, chief among them the death of her good friend Robin Anderson and her subsequent failed marriage to Robin's husband, Kim. After that, Stevie told *Us* magazine, "I moved to the beach for spiritual solace, for sanctuary. And it helped. For me to go out and just sit on a blanket and take my tape recorder and a pad of paper and a pencil and just look at the ocean and write. And give her (Robin) up, you know? And, you know if anything like that ever happens to me again, I'll probably move right back to the beach. Either that, or I'll go home to the desert. Because those two places are my strongholds."

In the July 14, 1991 *Boston Globe,* Stevie made this statement, "My mom says that God will never give you more than you can handle, and I really try hard to believe this, because sometimes I think I've been given more than I can handle. But it seems that I do have a real strong instinct to survive."

And, she could have added, not only to survive, but to turn the experiences of her own life, her thoughts, feelings, questions, and beliefs into music that all can share.

"I believe I was definitely sent down here to take people away for a little while, to make them

61

happy," she told Jenny Boyd for *Musicians In Tune*. "Every day I feel I have to do something, whether it's write a paragraph or sit at the piano for five minutes or go to the studio for a little while... I feel always that I have to hold up my end of the bargain, that I was given something by God, and He asks only that I give Him back something."

¤

Photo: Nancy Barr-Brandon

Sunday Break II
Labor Day Weekend, 1976
Austin, Texas

San Diego Arena
October 3, 1977

Photo: Nancy Barr-Brandon

Photo: Nancy Barr-Brandon

Photo: Joe Sia

Photo: Joe Sia

Photo: Nancy Barr-Brandon

Photo: Nancy Barr-Brandon

Photo: Joe Sia

85

S tevie Nicks is a poet of the heart, a romantic, a seeker looking for inspiration and meaning behind the sorrows of life. Her gift for transmitting deep feelings and searching questions through her music is an inspiration to her legions of fans and admirers.

The problems mankind faces in this period of history — depletion of the earth's resources, over-population, war, famine — seems to force us all to seek spiritual answers. Stevie Nicks is one of the searchers and poets of this age. There is surely a new age coming in whatever form it might take and Stevie Nicks will certainly remain at the forefront in the search for answers.

Maybe it was this impulse that led Stevie to compose a heartfelt letter to the troops involved in Operation Desert Storm during the Gulf War crisis, and to write the song *Desert Angel* for those fighting men and women. In her letter, published in the military newspaper *Stars and Stripes,* Stevie poured out her feelings of helplessness and talked about the beauty and hope embodied in the mythological figure of Rhiannon.

Stevie said that as she wrote she was clutching a "very large golden cross" which she wore around her neck, and sending "<u>that</u> energy" to them. She wrote that the cross bore her initials and the inscription "John 3:16." In drafting her letter, she drew the cross and in the space beside the drawing she wrote, "Yes, God so loved the world that He gave His only Son, that whoever believes in Him may not die but have eternal life." On a line underneath, she added, "Keep this in your hearts..."

Acknowledgements

This book is the result of more than two years of gathering material and research.

I, especially, want to thank all of Stevie's fans and the many Fan Clubs for their help and support.

Special thanks to Larry Shaeffer who's partnership on my first two books opened the way for this one.

Thanks to Charlie Jennemann and agent, Tony Secunda for start-up help. The book would not have come into existence without them.

Thanks to Jim Fox at Samuel French Trade and to Tom Newman at Impact Productions. Thanks to Jan Adams, Joe Sia, Michelle Rio, Bud Hart, Brad Zimmerman, John Galida (AKA John Thurston Twice), Inga Walton in Australia and Sue Cole in England.

Thanks to Paul Lutes (for putting us up in Phoenix on our way to Los Angeles), John Fitzgerald, Brent Maudlin, Don Bandel, Ed "Spider" Neidert, James Wincentsen & Katie, Marc Mathers, Virginia Lohle at Star File, Domenic Priore, David Leaf, Jim McDermott and a special thanks to the "Wild Hearts" on Prodigy for their support.

Thanks to all who I have not named or omitted by error. Thanks to all the fans who had the patience and endurance for the book to be completed even when I ran over schedule.

Thanks to all the artists and photographers who contributed, as well as all who helped with research. Thanks to J.E. for her help, "I remember our talks during research." May she be in peace.

Thanks to those who remain anonymous. And thanks to the subject of this book, Stevie Nicks. May there be many more books about her for her hungry fans and may this book help spur on Stevie to complete the book(s) she's mentioned for so long.

Illustration & Photo Credits

Photographers:

Joe Sia: Pages 57, 61, 67, 73, 81.

Nancy Barr-Brandon,
: Pages 16 (all four photos), 24 & 25 (all four photos), 28 (top two), 29 (top right), 42 & 43 (three), 46, 47 (bottom right), 54, 59, 62, 66 (two), 71, 75 (two), 77 (bottom), 85 (top).

© **George Kane**, Austin, TX: Pages 32, 34, 51, 64, 65 top).

Ralph Hulett: Pages 18, 28 (bottom), 29 (bottom), 31, 45, 50, 65 (bottom), 68, 69.

Don Bandel: Pages 29 (top left), 30, 36 (two), 47 (bottom left), 70, 82, 83

Jim Welander: Front cover photo, Pages 21 (two), 23, 26, 39-41 (all photos), 44, 47 (top), 48, 49, 84, 87.

Archives of Domenic Priore: Page 15.

Laura Boney (courtesy of): Page 58.

Dorothy A. Keveny: Page 77 (top).

Ed Wencentsen: Pages 86, 88.

Mike Palmer (UK): Pages 72, 78, 79.

Renae Ann Sauk: Page 74 (two).

Illustrators:

Johanna Pieterman: Page 1 (opposite Introduction), Pages, 12, 22, 46 (top left), 55.

Lisa Carrier (Nouveau Gypsy Illustrations): Pages 14, 19, 35, 38, 40, 42, 43, 48, 53, 56, 63, 72, 84 (top), 85 (top right).

Danielle Howell: Page 27.

Bill Tierney: Pages 76 (top), 80
2109 Carnelian Lane
Eagan, MN (55122) USA

Marc Mathers: Page 85 (bottom).

Resource Materials

Since I know fans are great collectors and like to find items of their favorite stars, I've compiled a list of the Fan Clubs, Fan publications, dealers, illustrators and photographers which I recommend.

Fan Clubs and Publications:

Frozen Love: Jolande Groenenboom
Elritsstraat 75
3192 CB Hoogvliet RT
The Netherlands

Silver Springs: P.O. Box 31091
Mesa, AZ (85275) USA

Dreaming Fairies: (Stevie/Kate Bush 'zine)
Peter Borbe]
Mindener Str 43
W-2841 Wagenfeld
Germany

Affairs of the Heart: Molendreef 10
461 CW Ossendrecht
The Netherlands

To write Stevie & Authorized Fan Club:
STEVIE NICKS
7605 Santa Monica Blvd #721
W. Hollywood, CA (90046) USA

For authentic Stevie items and autographed mechandise:

Silver Spring Emporium
102 S. Beeline Hwy.
Payson, AZ (85541) USA

Afterword

W E WERE crossing the long stretches of open road in the California desert after a harrowing trip through dangerous, icy winter roads in New Mexico in 1992. I was reading over my research material on Stevie Nicks for this book from materials I had received from many sources and my main book helper, Jean Enloe. Charlie Jennemann was my business associate, driving the car as I read.

The trip through the dangerous roads was unnerving to say the least. Many diesels lay on their sides along the road's edge, their tops split wide open like a fish that had been gutted. Boxes of their cargo spilled all alongside the wrecked vehicles. No drivers in sight, the diesels left there in the snow and ice storm abandoned like some dead animal. We had heard at a cafe that the roads ahead were dangerous, but there still was no confirmed reports yet and Charlie didn't want to lose time waiting out the storm.

We saw one car with a young couple ahead of us swing and swerve and finally lose control and cross over to the other side of the highway. Stuck in the snow and ice probably until the end of the storm. I was not relaxed for the whole stretch of eighty or ninety miles until we could reach Albuquerque and the elevation would be better. When we finally did reach Albuquerque the road conditions were better and we had come through the storm. I was finally able to relax once again and continue my research.

That material along with the two weeks of intense research with my helper, Jean Enloe, became the main contents of the first edition of this book. Since that time and other problems I was able to complete a second book on Stevie entitled, *Lady Of The Stars, Stevie Nicks*. In that book I went into more detail about the making of my first book.

Also, since the publication of the first book Stevie has released her latest solo album, *Street Angel*. It still remains to be seen how well the album sells, but that would not be the only way to measure it's success. Her big following of fans are now mostly happy to have a new album by Stevie and since she is an artist, art is not always measured by the income a piece of work brings in. I like the album very much and talk more about it in the second book. Stevie has had a good amount of press about the new album, some good, some bad. Her tour was well received, how it did in ticket sales I do not really know.

In *Rolling Stone Magazine*, September 22, 1994, Jancee Dunn asked how it had been on the road and Stevie replied, "I love being on the road. I'm going to be on a bus this time, which I've never done. I realized that since I don't go to sleep until 5 or 6 in the morning anyway, it's stupid for me to go home from a concert and sleep, because I can't. And my bus is so comfy."

Stevie is still the trooper, the continuing songwriter and performer. In answer to her critic of her continuing on with her career and if she is over the hill she replied in the U.K. publication, *Mojo*, in May of 1994, "I have no false illusions. I know that I'm like this little dinosaurette, truckin' and stompin' around. And you know every once in a while I have to come out and have tea with my fellow di-

97

nosaurettes, Ann & Nancy (Wilson) and Pat (Benatar). But I am not going anywhere. I've earned my place as an enduring woman in rock 'n' roll and I'm not about to give it up."

Modesty may not be one of Stevie's strongest characteristics, but survival is. She is still among us, still among the living. And when an artist is alive they must create. Stevie creates.

Stevie had her day with *Fleetwood Mac*, she proved that she could be a songwriter and did so with her beginning solo albums. After leaving Lindsey Buckingham, Mick and *Fleetwood Mac* she has continued on as a songwriter and performer. Will her latest work and future work compare to her things of the past? We will have to wait and see. But the mold is set. Stevie Nicks is an artist and she must create. I look forward to always hearing and seeing her work.

If one has a heart of a gypsy, a poet, a romantic, a dreamer and a visionary then I think that person will always be able to relate to the songwriting of Stevie Nicks. Her themes and storybook images will probably always remain in her songwriting. In Andy Warhol's magazine that he started, *Interview*, it was stated in the July 1994 issue, "Love, trust, and acceptance are the threads that neatly weave together on *Stevie Nicks'* latest release, *Street Angel* (Modern/Atlantic). The album combines Nicks' wrenching vocals with twangy country-rock guitar, creating a sound that's a complete departure from her work with Fleetwood Mac."

Some of Stevie's musical styles may change a little with the times, but this writer believes that she will always stay true to her unique vision of the world around her.

End

Photo by Nancy Barr-Brandon

Photo by Jim Welander

102

103

105

106

107

Wild ♡ Heart

Photo by Joe Sia

Photo by Star File

110

PHOTOS BY JOE SIA

<u>Award Winning Photographer</u>

- Rolling Stone Cover
- Rock Magazine Cover
- People Magazine Cover
- *Grand Funk Live!* Album
- John & Yoko/Plastic Ono Band w/ Elephant's Memory *Sometime in New York City* Album
- *Never A Dull Moment* Rod Stewart Album

<u>Published in More Than 47 Rock Books</u>

Send SASE for more Info:
Joe Sia
955 Tunxis Hill Road
Fairfield, CT (06430) USA

artwork
by
Johanna Pieterman

for info on stationary and prints:
Johanna Pieterman
c/o Pr. Julianastraat 22
4424 AV Wemeldinge
The Netherlands

**Photos of Over 100
Artists. SASE for
List. $2 Sample Photo**

— o —

**Ralph Hulett
P.O. Box 2304
Costa Mesa, CA 92628 USA**

Illustration by Johanna Pieterman

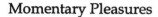

118

NEW THOUGHT JOURNAL

Vol. 1   No. 5

PHILOSOPHY • RELIGION • DIALOGUE • BOOK REVIEWS

$15 for one year
$3 for sample issue

NEW THOUGHT
JOURNAL

A new nationally distributed quarterly publication to inspire, challenge and enlighten the spirit within us all.

P.O. Box 700754
Tulsa, OK (74170) USA

Images of Jim Morrison is a collection of photographs of Morrison—on stage and off stage—Doors concert posters and handbills, and poems by Wincentsen and others that collectively evoke the memory of Jim Morrison.

$10.00 paper + $4 p/h
ISBN: 0-935839-11-9
94 pages, 6 x 9
Illus. (b & w and color)
Wynn Publishing
P.O. Box 1491
Pickens, SC (29671) USA

Images of
Jim Morrison

Edward Wincentsen

Also Available From Wynn Publishing!

LYNYRD SKYNYRD
"GIMME BACK MY BULLETS"
Original Concert UK Tour Book
(#11938) - $25.00

FLEETWOOD MAC
International Tribute/Commemorative Program
from '92 Austin Convention - ONLY 300 MADE!
(#20423) - $25.00

LED ZEPPELIN
AN EVENING WITH...
1977 Original Concert Tour Book
(#11937) - $20.00

JIM MORRISON
"IMAGES OF JIM MORRISON"
Book by Ed. Wincentsen
(#32421) - $10.00

STEVIE NICKS
"ROCK'S MYSTICAL LADY"
Revised Edition - Now 122 pages!
by Ed. Wincentsen
(#32422) - $15.00

STEVIE NICKS
"LADY OF THE STARS"
Book by Ed. Wincentsen
(#32423) - $15.00

EAGLES
1976 Original Concert Tour Book
(#11902) - $15.00

STEVIE NICKS
"WILD HEART"
Original Concert Tour Book
(#11953) - $75.00

STEVIE NICKS
High School Yearbook Reprint
ONLY 300 NUMBERED
COPIES
(#25643) - $35.00

STEVIE NICKS
"TIMESPACE"
Original Concert Tour Book
(#20041) - $30.00

STEVIE NICKS
"ROCK A LITTLE"
Original Concert Tour Book
(#11952) - $25.00

HEART
"PASSIONWORKS"
Original Concert Tour Book
(#11929) - $25.00

HEART
"BAD ANIMALS"
Original Concert Tour Book
(#11926) - $15.00

HEART
"BRIGADE"
Original Concert Tour Book
(#11928) - $15.00

OLIVIA NEWTON-JOHN
"PHYSICAL"
Original Concert Tour Book
(#11954) - $40.00

MADONNA
"BLONDE AMBITION"
Original Concert Tour Book
(#11940) - $20.00

MADONNA
"WHO'S THAT GIRL"
Original Concert Tour Book
(#11941) - $20.00

STEVIE NICKS
EUROPEAN IMPORT CALENDAR
11 3/4 x 16 1/2 Full Color
British Calendar
(#32424) - $15.00

STEVIE NICKS
"ROCK A LITTLE"
11x17 Original Concert Tour
Poster from Austin, TX
(#31619) - $12.00

STEVIE NICKS
"OTHER SIDE OF
THE MIRROR"
11x17 Original
Concert Tour Poster
from Austin, TX
(#31621) - $12.00

STEVIE NICKS
"WILD HEART"
11x17 Original Concert Tour
Poster from Austin, TX
(#31622) - $14.00

FLEETWOOD MAC
"RUMOURS"
Original Concert Tour Book
(#11914) - $50.00

Wynn Publishing books are available in many of the finer bookstores. If you have any difficulty
getting the book(s) you want, write to us at:

WYNN PUBLISHING
PO BOX 1491SB
PICKENS, SC
29671

List the items numbers and quantities you want. Please add $4 for Priority shipping or $6 for Insured Priority shipping
on any size order. South Carolina residents please add 5% sales tax. We accept Visa, MasterCard, Discover and
American Express. To place a phone order, please call us at 864-878-6469. To place a fax order, dial 864-878-6267.
Visit our web site at www.wynnco.com